Henry and Mudge
and
Mrs. Hopper's House

The Twenty-Second Book of Their Adventures

by Cynthia Rylant
illustrated by Carolyn Bracken
in the style of Suçie Stevenson

READY-TO-READ

ALADDIN PAPERBACKS
New York   London   Toronto   Sydney   Singapore

THE HENRY AND MUDGE BOOKS

First Aladdin Paperbacks edition January 2004

Text copyright © 2003 by Cynthia Rylant
Illustrations copyright © 2003 by Suçie Stevenson

ALADDIN PAPERBACKS
An imprint of Simon & Schuster Children's Publishing Division
1230 Avenue of the Americas
New York, NY 10020

Also available in a Simon & Schuster Books for Young Readers hardcover edition.
Book design by Mark Siegel
The text of this book was set in 18-point Goudy.
The illustrations are rendered in pen-and-ink and watercolor.
Printed in the United States of America
10

The Library of Congress has cataloged the hardcover edition as follows:
Rylant, Cynthia.
Henry and Mudge and Mrs. Hopper's House: the twenty-second book of their adventures / story by Cynthia
Rylant ; pictures by Suçie Stevenson.
p. cm. — (The Henry and Mudge books)
Summary: While Henry's parents are at a Sweetheart Dance on Valentine's Day, he and his dog Mudge have
a wonderful time staying at Mrs. Hopper's house, where they enjoy tea and music and dressing up in various
costumes.
ISBN 0-689-81153-5
[1. Babysitters—Fiction. 2. Costumes—Fiction. 3. Dogs—Fiction. 4. Valentine's Day—Fiction.]
I. Stevenson, Suçie, ill. II. Title. III. Series: Rylant, Cynthia. Henry and Mudge books.
PZ7.R982Heai 1999
[Fic]—dc21
98-20937
CIP
AC
ISBN 0-689-83446-2 (pbk.)
0511 LAK

Contents

FEBRUARY

4

A Sweetheart Dance

Valentine's Day was coming.

Henry and his big dog Mudge

loved Valentine's Day because of the

candy.

They liked the

little candy hearts

that said "You're swell" and "Oh, dear"

and things like that.

5

Henry read the words
and Mudge licked them off.
They were a good team.

On this Valentine's Day
Henry's father and Henry's mother
were going to
a Sweetheart Dance.

Henry and Mudge would be
staying with Mrs. Hopper.

8

Mrs. Hopper lived across the street
in a big stone house with droopy trees,
and dark windows,
and a gargoyle on the door.

Henry liked Mrs. Hopper.

But he did not like her house.
"Are you sure
Mudge and I can't come
to the Sweetheart Dance?"
Henry asked his father.

10

"Only if you both promise
to wear a tuxedo
and shiny black shoes
and waltz to 'The Blue Danube,'"
said Henry's father.

Henry looked at Mudge
and tried to imagine him in
a tuxedo and shiny black shoes,
waltzing to "The Blue Danube."

"I think we'd better go to Mrs. Hopper's,"
Henry said.

"Good idea," said Henry's father.

"Because Mudge only knows
how to tap-dance," Henry said with a grin.

Mrs. Hopper

On Valentine's night
Henry's parents got all dressed up.
Henry looked at them.
"Wow!" he said.
"I bet you didn't know
I was this handsome,"
said Henry's dad.

15

"*I did*," said Henry's mother,
giving him a kiss.

"Ugh, too much mushy stuff,"
Henry said to Mudge.

"Let's get to Mrs. Hopper's
house *quick!*"

At Mrs. Hopper's house
Mudge licked the
gargoyle on the front door.
Henry giggled.
"He didn't scare *you*,
Mudge," Henry said.

18

When Mrs. Hopper opened the door,
she had a violin in her hand.
She smiled at Henry.
She petted Mudge.

She said good-bye to
Henry's parents,
and Henry and Mudge
went inside.

"Wow!" said Henry.

He had never been
inside Mrs. Hopper's house
before.
It was like a castle.

There were big chandeliers

and tall paintings

and a grand piano.

And, lucky for Mudge, *cats everywhere!*

23

"How many cats do you
have, Mrs. Hopper?"
asked Henry.
"Eleven," said Mrs. Hopper.
"All girls."

Mudge looked at the
cats and wagged.

"Mudge loves cats,"
Henry told Mrs. Hopper.
Mrs. Hopper petted
Mudge again.
"Mudge loves everything,"
she said.
Henry smiled.
Mrs. Hopper's house
wasn't bad.
It was wonderful.

Maybe his parents

would dance all night long.

27

Costumes

Mrs. Hopper wasn't like
anyone Henry had ever met.
She played the violin for him.
She served him tea.
She told him about her father,
who had been
a famous actor.

29

She was very kind to Mudge.
She cooked him a
bowl of oatmeal and
gave him his own loaf
of French bread.

After the tea and music and oatmeal

Mrs. Hopper took them upstairs.

She opened a room
that had been her father's.
"Wow!" said Henry.
The room was full of costumes.

There were silk capes
and tall hats
and shiny coats.

There were canes

and swords and umbrellas.

There were wigs.

Mrs. Hopper put a
wig on Mudge.
"You look like a poodle, Mudge!"
said Henry.
Mudge wagged and wagged.

Henry and Mudge
and Mrs. Hopper spent
most of the evening
in the costume room.
They had a wonderful time.

And when Henry's parents
came back from the dance,
were they ever surprised.

Mudge was a poodle
and Henry was a man!
Henry wore a tuxedo
and a hat
and shiny black shoes.

39

"I bet you didn't know
I was this handsome,"
Henry told his dad.
And everyone
40   laughed and laughed.